A *homeless* Christmas Story

Written by **Ryan Dowd**

Illustrated by **Bradley H. Clark**

Winter's crisp darkness settled over the
large, brick homeless shelter.

Chicago winds whooshed snow across a
frozen parking lot.

*Christmas Eves at homeless shelters are
not very different from other nights.*
Volunteers from a local church carried
trays of steaming spaghetti inside. A
hundred hungry women, children and
men dressed in tattered coats stood
around outside, waiting for the shelter to
open for dinner.

Nearby, a lone man shuffled toward the shelter slowly—
carefully—over an icy sidewalk. His massive boots made
a soft crunching sound on frozen salt crystals.

The man's coat and hat—while heavy—were unable to
block the biting chill of this cold winter night.

At least his long, tangled beard kept his face warm.
People often stared at his beard and clothing. It had
taken time, but he had grown used to people staring. In
fact, he barely even noticed anymore.

When the man reached the shelter, he dropped a black garbage bag in the snow. No one noticed. *A man carrying a garbage bag of belongings is a common sight at a homeless shelter.*

A woman in a coat four sizes too large smiled at the man and offered a broken candy cane. He politely declined, rubbing his hands together to keep warm.

Finally, the door to the shelter opened and everyone formed a line to go inside. The line moved like molasses. Some people had lost their shelter ID cards. Others paused for a weary staff member to wave a metal detector at their overstuffed pockets.

The man with the heavy coat and long beard waited patiently. When it was his turn, the staff member greeted him by name and welcomed him in with a tired smile and sincere "Merry Christmas."

The man heaved his heavy, drained body into the warmth. His thick boots tracked dirty snow inside.

Fluorescent lights buzzed overhead, casting harsh light onto rows of tables stuffed into the room. Different smells—some pleasant, others not—filled the air. Sugary, buttery cookies and strong, black coffee were the strongest.

A volunteer approached the man. The woman was elderly, thin, and wore a sweater with a reindeer on it. She greeted him with a tray of drinks in Styrofoam cups: decaf coffee or orange Kool-Aid. The man picked up a cup of coffee and took a sip. It was too strong, bitter and hot, but instantly he felt warmer as the rich dark coffee warmed him from the inside.

The man nodded to people he knew. This was not his first night at a shelter. He had been coming for years... many years... far too many years.

He vividly remembered last Christmas Eve here. And the year before... and the year before that, and...

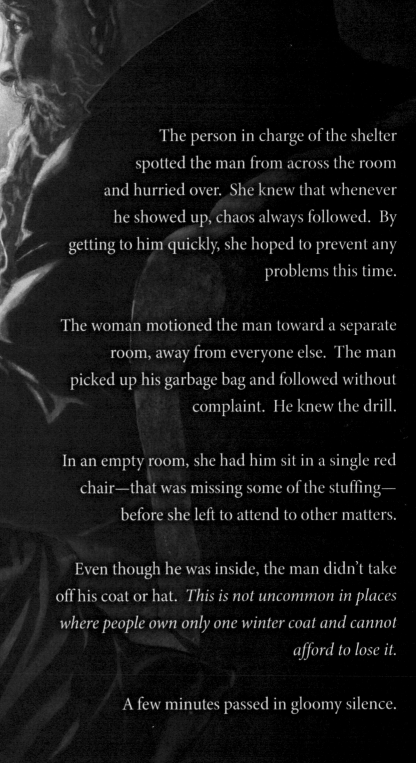

The person in charge of the shelter spotted the man from across the room and hurried over. She knew that whenever he showed up, chaos always followed. By getting to him quickly, she hoped to prevent any problems this time.

The woman motioned the man toward a separate room, away from everyone else. The man picked up his garbage bag and followed without complaint. He knew the drill.

In an empty room, she had him sit in a single red chair—that was missing some of the stuffing— before she left to attend to other matters.

Even though he was inside, the man didn't take off his coat or hat. *This is not uncommon in places where people own only one winter coat and cannot afford to lose it.*

A few minutes passed in gloomy silence.

A young girl—about five years old, with curly dark hair and brown eyes—wandered into the room by herself. She was eating a cookie shaped like a Christmas tree decorated with thick green frosting.

The man looked up at the little girl, expecting to see fear in her eyes. Children were often afraid of him. *Children living in homeless shelters, though, grow comfortable around strangers because of the thousands of volunteers.*

The little girl—green frosting squishing between her fingers—walked right up to the man. She noticed that he had a sorrowful look on his face. As much time as he had spent in homeless shelters, seeing children living in them still made him sad.

It was clear to the girl that the man was trying to hide his feelings from everyone.

She understood what that was like.

A boisterous commotion broke
out in the hallway behind the girl,
but she didn't notice. *Shelters
are noisy places.* It moved closer,
but the little girl just stood there.
Suddenly, a dozen young children
tumbled into the room, trailed by
an overwhelmed staff person.

The children froze when they saw
the man, their eyes wide.

He sat up straight...
took a deep breath...
and yelled at them...

"Ho! Ho! Ho! Merry Christmas!"

The little brown-haired girl crawled onto the man's lap. Presents wrapped in shimmering paper with colorful bows spilled from the garbage bag. The other children giggled, scrambling to form a line.

Looking up at the man, the little girl asked, **"What do YOU want for Christmas?"**

He was silent. He imagined a world without homelessness. A world without shelters. A world where every child—every person—has a home.

A smile slowly spread across the little girl's face as she understood.

"Me too. That's what I want too, Santa."

Dear Reader,

I started volunteering at the homeless shelter featured in this story—Hesed House in Aurora, Illinois—when I was thirteen years old. I immediately knew it was a special place... even if my adolescent self could not yet explain why.

I was fortunate enough to join the staff during college and become Executive Director after law school.

Over the last few decades, I've spent many Christmas Eves at the shelter.

Just like Santa in the story, I cannot get used to seeing children living in a homeless shelter. Obviously, no one of any age should experience homelessness. The sight of children, though, cuts through our flimsy excuses for allowing homelessness to exist.

It is possible, by the way...
We CAN end homelessness.

Homelessness—as we understand it today—is a recent development. It started in the 1980s. If we created homelessness since I was born, I don't think it is unreasonable to ask that we end it before I die.

We have all the tools we need to banish homelessness to the history books.

So, what's stopping us?

What will it take to end homelessness?

It will take hope... We must have hope, but not the hope of naïve fools and untested daydreamers.

The kind of hope that changes the world is born in experience; it has scars from battles won and battles lost. It is weary and ragged, but unbroken. Always unbroken.

It will take impatience...
We must grow impatient with a status quo that accepts dehumanization as the inevitable consequence of modernity.

We will remake the world only when our souls can no longer bear to witness the unnecessary suffering of others.

It will take courage...
We must have the courage to reject the cynicism that grips our world and whispers in our ears, "You don't matter."

Such cynicism is worse than cowardice because it robs our generation—and future generations—of possibility.

It will take sacrifice...
We must accept that the world will not be saved through our social media posts.

Real change requires the real sacrifices of real people willing to challenge very real systemic injustice and political inertia.

We <u>will</u> end homelessness, but only when we want to badly enough.

And when we do, I hope my own story ends similarly to this book:

> *My great-granddaughter climbs up on my lap and asks, "Gramp-Gramp, what was Hesed House?"*
>
> *I rub my long white beard and say, "Hesed House was a homeless shelter."*
>
> *With total innocence she asks, "What's a homeless shelter?"*
>
> *"Well, dear," I sigh, taking a deep breath, "there used to be people in our community who didn't have a home to live in...*
>
> *...but that was before you were born."*

Humanity is worth the struggle... We are worth the struggle...

Peace,
Ryan Dowd

ABOUT THE AUTHOR

Ryan Dowd spent most of his career as Executive Director of Hesed House. He is still on the staff, but now spends most of his time educating the world about homelessness through his company, Empathy Studios.

This is Ryan's second book and eighth publication. The Librarian's Guide to Homelessness is one of the American Library Association's most successful publications. Ryan—a lawyer—has also had articles published in legal journals, covering homeless education rights and how modern legal ethics harm individuals living in poverty.

Ryan's favorite book is Dharma Bums by Jack Kerouac. He started reading it as a freshman in college and has been reading it on and off ever since. The trick is to immediately start back on page one after finishing it!

Ryan is ecstatically married to Krissie, his business and life partner and is the overly proud father of Cameron and Hailey.

ABOUT THE ILLUSTRATOR

Bradley H. Clark considers himself a lucky man having been able to do what he loves, painting professionally, for over 30 years.

Born and raised in the big landscapes and farmland of Idaho, he was educated at Brigham Young University and Art Center College of Design. Upon graduation he married Cynthia Watts, a classmate, and they moved to NYC to pursue art careers together. Later they relocated to the Hudson Valley of New York to raise three children. He currently resides in Salt Lake City, Utah, where he moved to pursue another passion - vocal music. He sings with the Mormon Tabernacle Choir, Utah Chamber Artists and the Utah Symphony Chorus.

Bradley would like to dedicate this book to his three grandchildren, Skyler, Audrey, and Matheo, and encourage them to always be empathetic to people and strive to be aware of opportunities for service.

Bradley's website is www.BradleyClarkArt.com.

ABOUT HESED HOUSE

Hesed House is the second largest homeless shelter in Illinois. It is so much more than just a homeless shelter, though.

Hesed House helped pioneer the model of the "comprehensive homeless resource center," which offers everything a person needs to get out of homelessness. It offers onsite mental health counseling, substance abuse counseling, a medical clinic, a legal clinic, veteran's services and much more.

In an average week, sixteen individuals arrive at Hesed House newly homeless. In an average week, sixteen individuals move out into their own housing. Every staff member, board member and volunteer is working frantically to get seventeen (or more) people out per week!

For more information (or to donate), please go to www.HesedHouse.org

ABOUT EMPATHY STUDIOS

Empathy Studios trains organizations how to compassionately manage problematic behavior from individuals experiencing homelessness.

The trainings are embraced by shelters, libraries, police departments, local governments and businesses around the world. They are especially popular, though, in the United States, Canada, Australia, New Zealand and Brazil.

Empathy Studios was founded by Ryan and Krissie Dowd.

For more information, go to www.HomelessTraining.com.

CPSIA information can be obtained
at www.ICGtesting.com
Printed in the USA
LVHW072057051122
732457LV00008B/95